KU-134-545

Carl Sandburg

ROOTABAGA STORIES

Illustrated by
Maud Petersham and Miska Petersham

Edited by Jonathan Cott

BAREFOOT BOOKS
Boston & Bath
1994

Barefoot Books
Horticultural Hall
300 Massachusetts Avenue
Boston, Massachusetts 02115

Barefoot Books Ltd
P.O. Box 95
Kingswood, Bristol 5BH

9 8 7 6 5 4 3 2 1

First Barefoot Books Edition

Series designed by Dede Cummings/IPA
Printed in Singapore on acid-free paper ∞

Distributed in the United States by
Random House, Inc., and in Canada
by Random House of Canada Ltd

See page 167 for Library of Congress
Cataloging-in-Publication data.

CONTENTS

CARL SANDBURG lived the life of an American folk hero. Born in 1873 of semiliterate Swedish immigrants, he was raised in the prairie town of Galesburg, Illinois. At thirteen, he quit school, rode freight trains as a hobo, and later fought in the Spanish-American War and worked as a journalist and political activist. With the 1916 publication of his *Chicago Poems,* Sandburg took on the mantle of poet laureate of the city he heralded as "Hog Butcher for the World, Tool Maker, Stacker of Wheat, Player with Railroads and Freight Handler to the Nation." A forerunner of Woody

Guthrie and Bob Dylan, he spent much of his life traveling throughout the United States with his guitar, collecting and singing for delighted audiences such folk songs and ballads as "Foggy, Foggy Dew" and "Barbara Allen," which he would later publish in his milestone collection, *The American Songbag* (1927). By the time of his death in 1967, Sandburg had been lionized by several American presidents and had received a score of honorary doctorates and two Pulitzer Prizes for his *Collected Poems* and his multivolume biography of Abraham Lincoln. But perhaps his most enduring achievement was his remarkable creation of the imaginary realm he called Rootabaga Country.

Sandburg described this fictional world and its inhabitants in two books, *Rootabaga Stories* (1922) and *Rootabaga*

Pigeons (1923), which were intended, the author once asserted, "for people from 5 to 105 years of age." (In 1993, ten additional Rootabaga stories were published under the title *More Rootabagas*.) In truth, the stories were elaborations and distillations of tales—known to the family as "corn fairy" stories—that Sandburg had begun improvising several years earlier for, at first, his two oldest daughters, Margaret and Janet (nicknamed Spink and Skabootch, to whom he dedicated the first volume), and, later, his youngest child, Helga (including her in his dedication of the second volume to "Three Illinois Pigeons"). "I was tired of princes and princesses," he explained, "and I sought the American equivalent of elves and gnomes. I knew that American children would respond, so I wrote some nonsense tales with American fooling in them."

A rutabaga is a large yellow Swedish turnip; its name is derived from the Swedish words for "a baggy or mis-shapen root." Sandburg turned the Swedish *rut* into the American *root,* thereby capturing its original meaning, and announcing both a new word and a new world. Rootabaga Country has its roots, of course, in the American Midwest; but it is a Midwest that seems to be floating and shimmering above the ordinary one, in another dimension that is both nonsensical and paradisiacal.

To the east of the Shampoo River and the Big Lake of the Booming Rollers, Rootabaga farmers harvest wheat, hay, and corn with the help of corn fairies, and they plant crops of balloons with strings for roots. Flummywister birds yodel their yisters in the long branches of the lingering leaves. Young frogs shoot silver spears of little new songs up into the sky. Zigzagging insects called zizzy bugs, with little hizzers on their heads and legs, construct the dizzying Zigzag Railroad.

Meanwhile, back in the Village of Liver-and-Onions—"the biggest city in the big, big Rootabaga Country"— the Potato Face Blind Man plays his gold-that-used-to-be accordion in front of the Main Street post office, wearing a sign that says "I Am Blind *Too*," explaining that people "look where they are going and they get where they wish to get, but they forget why they came and they do not know how to come away. They are my blind brothers." Nearby, two skyscrapers across the street from each other lean over and whisper to each other at night and eventually decide to have a baby ("It must be a *free* child," they declare, ". . . free to run across the prairie, to the mountains, to the sea"), and they give birth to the Golden Spike Limited, the fastest long distance train in Rootabaga Country.

Walt Whitman once described his *Leaves of Grass* as "only a language experiment . . . an attempt to give the spirit, the body, the man, new words, new potentialities of speech—an American . . . range of self-expression. . . . Because what is America for? To commemorate the old myths and the gods? To repeat the Mediterranean here? Or the uses and growths of Europe here? No . . . but to destroy all those from the purposes of the earth, and to erect a new earth in their place."

As one of the truest exponents of the

Whitmanian experiment, Carl Sandburg succeeded in erecting this "new earth," not so much in his enormous body of poetry, which often seems overly mawkish, sentimental, and magniloquent, but rather in his Rootabaga stories, often overlooked or derogated because of their status as "merely" children's literature.

"I'm going to do a Kid book," Sandburg announced to a friend before starting *Rootabaga Stories*. "They are the anarchs of language and speech and we'll have a lot of fun, whether it's a real book or not." In fact, Sandburg admitted later, the writing of those stories was the hardest work he had ever done, commenting, "They've got my best blood and heartbeats and breath." And to a children's book editor he further elaborated, "They were attempts to catch fantasy, accents, pulses, eye flashes, inconceivably rapid and perfect gestures, sudden pantomimic moments, drawls and drolleries, gazings and musings—authoritative poetic instants—knowing that if the whirr of them were caught quickly and simply enough the result would be a child lore interesting to child and grownup."

The author knew exactly what he was about. The Rootagaba stories are a veritable *Song of My (Child) Self*, with Sandburg's uncanny sensitivity to the sound-meaning and touch-meaning of words that children everywhere are so enamored with and his mastery of the American idiom. (Sandburg, like Whitman, used to walk around and fill his notebooks with scintillating examples of overheard everyday expressions, phrases, and epithets—what Whitman called "miracles of the mouth.")

Sandburg, moreover, being also a guitarist and singer, reveals his profound knowledge of folk music, blues, and jazz in every riff, turn, break, refrain, and chorus of his truly swinging, sighing, and wailing Rootabaga texts. His appreciation of Native American mythology inspired him to write two of his most beautiful stories, "The White Horse Girl and the Blue Wind Boy" and "Sand Flat Shadows." And his passion for American film comedies—especially those of Charlie Chaplin—is evident in tale after tale. As a movie critic for the *Chicago Daily News,* Sandburg met Chaplin in Hollywood in 1921, and later wrote him to ask if he might consider writing a preface for *Rootabaga Stories.* Chaplin never replied. But the comedian's spirit is everywhere embodied in the inhabitants of Rootabaga Country—Dippy the

Wisp, Bimbo the Snip, Johnny the Wham, Joe the Wimp, and, of course, the Potato Face Blind Man.

When *Rootabaga Stories* first appeared, Sandburg received a letter from an irate parent in Newark, New Jersey:

> At breakfast this morning my daughter Grace, who is seven years old, called her little sister a "dirty sniveling snitch." Upon inquiry I found that Grace had picked up this highly elevating denunciation from a book which her mother had assured her was highly recommended and would prove amusing. Perusal of [your] book by myself left me in a quandary. Do you consider such phrases as "Sap-head" and "home-thief" literature for children?

But with the exception of a few similarly squeamish parents, *Rootabaga Sto-*

ries quickly won a devoted audience. May Massee, a Chicago book editor, wrote: "Why, that old Potato Face Blind Man is as wise as Socrates and a deal more companionable." Georgia O'Keeffe insisted that her husband Alfred Stieglitz stop what he was doing and immediately sit down to listen to her read aloud the story "How the Five Rusty Rats Helped Find a New Village." And at Taliesin, Frank Lloyd Wright's young architectural associates put on marionette productions based on the Rootabaga stories for their own entertainment. Wright himself wrote to Sandburg, "I read your fairy tales nearly every night before I go to bed. They fill a long-felt want—Poetry. I'll soon know them all by heart. . . . All the children that will be born into the Middle West during the next hundred years are peeping at you now, Carl—

between little pink fingers—smiling, knowing in their hearts they have found a friend."

This selection of tales from *Rootabaga Stories* (1922) and *Rootabaga Pigeons* (1923) appears here with the original illustrations by the renowned wife-and-husband collaborators Maud and Miska Petersham.

JONATHAN COTT
Series Editor

ROOTABAGA
STORIES

How They Broke Away to Go to the Rootabaga Country

G IMME the Ax lived in a house where everything is the same as it always was.

"The chimney sits on top of the house and lets the smoke out," said Gimme the Ax. "The doorknobs open the doors. The windows are always either open or shut. We are always either upstairs or downstairs in this house. Everything is the same as it always was."

So he decided to let his children name themselves.

"The first words they speak as soon as they learn to make words shall be their names," he said. "They shall name themselves."

When the first boy came to the house of Gimme the Ax, he was named Please Gimme. When the first girl came she was named Ax Me No Questions.

And both of the children had the shadows of valleys by night in their eyes and the lights of early morning, when the sun is coming up, on their foreheads.

And the hair on top of their heads

was a dark wild grass. And they loved to turn the doorknobs, open the doors, and run out to have the wind comb their hair and touch their eyes and put its six soft fingers on their foreheads.

And then because no more boys came and no more girls came, Gimme the Ax said to himself, "My first boy is my last and my last girl is my first and they picked their names themselves."

Please Gimme grew up and his ears got longer. Ax Me No Questions grew up and her ears got longer. And they kept on living in the house where everything is the same as it always was. They learned to say just as their father said, "The chimney sits on top of the house and lets the smoke out, the doorknobs open the doors, the windows are always either open or shut, we are always either upstairs or downstairs—everything is the same as it always was."

After a while they began asking each other in the cool of the evening after they had eggs for breakfast in the morning, "Who's who? How much? And what's the answer?"

"It is too much to be too long anywhere," said the tough old man, Gimme the Ax.

And Please Gimme and Ax Me No Questions, the tough son and the tough daughter of Gimme the Ax, answered their father, "It *is* too much to be too long anywhere."

So they sold everything they had, pigs, pastures, pepper pickers, pitchforks, everything except their ragbags and a few extras.

When their neighbors saw them selling everything they had, the different neighbors said, "They are going to

Kansas, to Kokomo, to Canada, to Kankakee, to Kalamazoo, to Kamchatka, to the Chattahoochee."

One little sniffer with his eyes half shut and a mitten on his nose, laughed in his hat five ways and said, "They are going to the moon and when they get there they will find everything is the same as it always was."

All the spot cash money he got for selling everything, pigs, pastures, pepper pickers, pitchforks, Gimme the Ax put in a ragbag and slung on his back like a rag picker going home.

Then he took Please Gimme, his oldest and youngest and only son, and Ax Me No Questions, his oldest and youngest and only daughter, and went to the railroad station.

The ticket agent was sitting at the window selling railroad tickets the same as always.

"Do you wish a ticket to go away and come back or do you wish a ticket to go away and *never* come back?" the ticket agent asked wiping sleep out of his eyes.

"We wish a ticket to ride where the railroad tracks run off into the sky and never come back—send us far as the railroad rails go and then forty ways farther yet," was the reply of Gimme the Ax.

"So far? So early? So soon?" asked the ticket agent wiping more sleep out his eyes. "Then I will give you a new ticket. It blew in. It is a long slick yellow leather slab ticket with a blue spanch across it."

Gimme the Ax thanked the ticket agent once, thanked the ticket agent twice, and then instead of thanking the ticket agent three times he opened the ragbag and took out all the spot cash

He opened the ragbag and took out all the spot cash money.

money he got for selling everything, pigs, pastures, pepper pickers, pitchforks, and paid the spot cash money to the ticket agent.

Before he put it in his pocket he looked once, twice, three times at the long yellow leather slab ticket with a blue spanch across it.

Then with Please Gimme and Ax Me No Questions he got on the railroad train, showed the conductor his ticket and they started to ride to where the railroad tracks run off into the blue sky and then forty ways farther yet.

The train ran on and on. It came to the place where the railroad tracks run off into the blue sky. And it ran on and on chick chick-a-chick chick-a-chick chick-a-chick.

Sometimes the engineer hooted and tooted the whistle. Sometimes the fireman rang the bell. Sometimes the open-and-shut of the steam hog's nose choked and spit pfisty-pfoost, pfisty-pfoost, pfisty-pfoost. But no matter what happened to the whistle and the bell and the steam hog, the train ran on and on to where the railroad tracks run off into the blue sky. And then it ran on and on more and more.

Sometimes Gimme the Ax looked in his pocket, put his fingers in and took out the long slick yellow leather slab ticket with a blue spanch across it.

"Not even the Kings of Egypt with all their climbing camels, and all their speedy, spotted, lucky lizards, ever had a ride like this," he said to his children.

Then something happened. They met another train running on the same track. One train was going one way. The other was going the other way. They met. They passed each other.

"What was it—what happened?" the children asked their father.

"One train went over, the other train went under," he answered. "This is the Over and Under Country. Nobody gets out of the way of anybody else. They either go over or under."

Next they came to the country of the balloon pickers. Hanging down from the sky strung on strings so fine the eye could not see them at first, was the balloon crop of that summer. The sky was thick with balloons. Red, blue, yellow balloons, white, purple, and orange balloons—peach, watermelon, and potato balloons—rye loaf and wheat loaf balloons—link sausage and pork chop balloons—they floated and filled the sky.

The balloon pickers were walking on high stilts picking balloons. Each picker had his own stilts, long or short.

For picking balloons near the ground he had short stilts. If he wanted to pick far and high he walked on a far and high pair of stilts.

Baby pickers on baby stilts were picking baby balloons. When they fell off the stilts the handful of balloons they were holding kept them in the air till they got their feet into the stilts again.

"Who is that away up there in the sky climbing like a bird in the morning?" Ax Me No Questions asked her father.

"He was singing too happy," replied the father. "The songs came out of his neck and made him so light the balloons pulled him off his stilts."

"Will he ever come down again back to his own people?"

"Yes, his heart will get heavy when

his songs are all gone. Then he will drop down to his stilts again."

The train was running on and on. The engineer hooted and tooted the whistle when he felt like it. The fireman rang the bell when he felt that way. And sometimes the open-and-shut of the steam hog had to go pfisty-pfoost, pfisty-pfoost.

"Next is the country where the circus clowns come from," said Gimme the Ax to his son and daughter. "Keep your eyes open."

They did keep their eyes open. They saw cities with ovens, long and short ovens, fat stubby ovens, lean lank ovens, all for baking either long or short clowns, or fat and stubby or lean and lank clowns.

After each clown was baked in the oven it was taken out into the sunshine and put up to stand like a big white doll with a red mouth leaning against the fence.

Two men came along to each baked clown standing still like a doll. One man threw a bucket of white fire over it. The second man pumped a wind pump with a living red wind through the red mouth.

The clown rubbed his eyes, opened his mouth, twisted his neck, wiggled his ears, wriggled his toes, jumped away from the fence and began turning handsprings, cartwheels, somersaults and flipflops in the sawdust ring near the fence.

"The next we come to is the Rootabaga Country where the big city is the Village of Liver-and-Onions," said Gimme the Ax, looking again in his pocket to be sure he had the long slick yellow leather slab ticket with a blue spanch across it.

The train ran on and on till it stopped running straight and began running in zigzags like one letter Z put next to another Z and the next and the next.

The tracks and the rails and the ties and the spikes under the train all stopped being straight and changed to zigzags like one letter Z and another letter Z put next after the other.

"It seems like we go half way and then back up," said Ax Me No Questions.

"Look out of the window and see if the pigs have bibs on," said Gimme the Ax. "If the pigs are wearing bibs then this is the Rootabaga Country."

And they looked out of the zigzagging windows of the zigzagging cars and the first pigs they saw had bibs on. And the next pigs and the next pigs they saw all had bibs on.

The checker pigs had checker bibs on, the striped pigs had striped bibs on. And the polka dot pigs had polka dot bibs on.

"Who fixes it for the pigs to have bibs on?" Please Gimme asked his father.

"The fathers and mothers fix it," answered Gimme the Ax. "The checker pigs have checker fathers and mothers. The striped pigs have striped fathers and mothers. And the polka dot pigs have polka dot fathers and mothers."

And the train went zigzagging on and on running on the tracks and the rails and the spikes and the ties which were all zigzag like the letter Z and the letter Z.

And after a while the train zigzagged on into the Village of Liver-and-

Onions, known as the biggest city in the big, big Rootabaga Country.

And so if you are going to the Rootabaga Country you will know when you get there because the railroad tracks change from straight to zigzag, the pigs have bibs on, and it is the fathers and mothers who fix it.

And if you start to go to that country remember first you must sell everything you have, pigs, pastures, pepper pickers, pitchforks, put the spot cash money in a ragbag and go to the railroad station and ask the ticket agent for a long slick yellow leather slab ticket with a blue spanch across it.

And you mustn't be surprised if the ticket agent wipes sleep from his eyes and asks, "So far? So early? So soon?"

How the Five Rusty Rats
Helped Find a New Village

ONE day while Wing Tip the Spick was visiting her four uncles in the Village of Liver-and-Onions, a blizzard came up. Snow filled the sky and the wind blew and made a noise like heavy wagon axles grinding and crying.

And on this day a gray rat came to the house of the four uncles, a rat with gray skin and gray hair, gray as the gray gravy on a beefsteak. The rat had a basket. In the basket was a catfish. And the rat said, "Please let me have a little fire and a little salt as I wish to make a little bowl of hot catfish soup to keep me warm through the blizzard."

And the four uncles all said together, "This is no time for rats to be around—and we would like to ask you where you got the catfish in the basket."

"Oh, oh, oh, please—in the name of the five rusty rats, the five lucky rats of the Village of Cream Puffs, please don't," was the exclamation of Wing Tip the Spick.

The uncles stopped. They looked long and deep into the eyes of Wing Tip the Spick and thought, as they had thought before, how her eyes were clear light blue, the same as cornflowers with blue raindrops shining on the silver leaves in a summer sun shower.

And the four uncles opened the door and let the gray rat come in with the basket and the catfish. They showed the gray rat the way to the kitchen and the fire and the salt. And they watched the rat and kept him company while he fixed himself a catfish soup to keep him warm traveling through the blizzard with the sky full of snow.

After they opened the front door and let the rat out and said good-by, they turned to Wing Tip the Spick and asked her to tell them about the five rusty lucky rats of the Village of Cream Puffs where she lived with her father and her mother and her folks.

"When I was a little girl growing

up, before I learned all I learned since I got older, my grandfather gave me a birthday present because I was nine years old. I remember how he said to me, 'You will never be nine years old again after this birthday, so I give you this box for a birthday present.'

"In the box was a pair of red slippers with a gold clock on each slipper. One of the clocks ran fast. The other clock ran slow. And he told me if I wished to be early anywhere I should go by the clock that ran fast. And if I wished to be late anywhere I should go by the clock that ran slow.

"And that same birthday he took me down through the middle of the Village of Cream Puffs to the public square near the Roundhouse of the Big Spool. There he pointed his finger at the statue of the five rusty rats, the

five lucky rats. And as near as I can remember his words, he said:

" 'Many years ago, long before the
snow birds began to wear funny little
slip-on hats and funny little slip-on
shoes, and away back long before the
snow birds learned how to slip off their
slip-on hats and how to slip off their
slip-on shoes, long ago in the faraway
Village of Liver-and-Onions, the people who ate cream puffs came together
and met in the streets and picked up
their baggage and put their belongings
on their shoulders and marched out of
the Village of Liver-and-Onions saying, "We shall find a new place for a
village and the name of it shall be the
Village of Cream Puffs."

" 'They marched out on the prairie
with their baggage and belongings in
sacks on their shoulders. And a blizzard
came up. Snow filled the sky. The

wind blew and blew and made a noise like heavy wagon axles grinding and crying.

" 'The snow came on. The wind twisted all day and all night and all the next day. The wind changed black and twisted and spit icicles in their faces. They got lost in the blizzard. They expected to die and be buried in the snow for the wolves to come and eat them.

" 'Then the five lucky rats came, the five rusty rats, rust on their skin and hair, rust on their feet and noses, rust all over, and especially, most especially of all, rust on their long curved tails. They dug their noses down into the snow and their long curved tails stuck up far above the snow where the people who were lost in the blizzard could take hold of the tails like handles.

" 'And so, while the wind and the

They held on to the long curved tails of the rusty rats.

snow blew and the blizzard beat its icicles in their faces, they held on to the long curved tails of the rusty rats till they came to the place where the Village of Cream Puffs now stands. It was the rusty rats who saved their lives and showed them where to put their new village. That is why this statue now stands in the public square, this statue of the shapes of the five rusty rats, the five lucky rats with their noses down in the snow and their long curved tails lifted high out of the snow.'

"That is the story as my grandfather told it to me. And he said it happened long ago, long before the snow birds began to wear slip-on hats and slip-on shoes, long before they learned how to slip off the slip-on hats and to slip off the slip-on shoes."

"O-h-h-h," said one of the uncles.

"Um-m-m-m," said the other three uncles.

"And sometime," added Wing Tip the Spick, "when you get away from the Village of Liver-and-Onions and cross the Shampoo River and ride many miles across the upland prairie till you come to the Village of Cream Puffs, you will find a girl there who loves four uncles very much.

"And if you ask her politely, she will show you the red slippers with gold clocks on them, one clock to be early by, the other to be late by. And if you are still more polite she will take you

through the middle of the town to the
public square and show you the statue
of the five rusty lucky rats with their
long curved tails sticking up in the air
like handles. And the tails are curved
so long and so nice you will feel like
going up and taking hold of them to
see what will happen to you."

The Potato Face Blind Man Who Lost the Diamond Rabbit on His Gold Accordion

THERE was a Potato Face Blind Man used to play an accordion on the Main Street corner nearest the post office in the Village of Liver-and-Onions.

Any Ice Today came along and said, "It looks like it used to be an 18 carat gold accordion with rich pawnshop diamonds in it; it looks like it used to be a grand accordion once and not so grand now."

"Oh, yes, oh, yes, it was gold all over on the outside," said the Potato Face Blind Man, "and there was a diamond rabbit next to the handles on each side, two diamond rabbits."

"How do you mean diamond rabbits?" Any Ice Today asked.

"Ears, legs, head, feet, ribs, tail, all fixed out in diamonds to make a nice rabbit with his diamond chin on his diamond toenails. When I play good pieces so people cry hearing my accordion music, then I put my fingers over and feel of the rabbit's diamond chin on his diamond toenails, 'Attaboy, li'l bunny, attaboy, li'l bunny.'"

"Yes I hear you talking but it is like dream talking. I wonder why your accordion looks like somebody stole it and took it to a pawnshop and took it out and somebody stole it again and took it to a pawnshop and took it out and somebody stole it again. And they kept on stealing it and taking it out of the pawnshop and stealing it again till the gold wore off so it looks like a used-to-be-yesterday."

"Oh, yes, o-h, y-e-s, you are right. It is not like the accordion it used to be. It knows more knowledge than it used to know just the same as this Potato Face Blind Man knows more knowledge than he used to know."

"Tell me about it," said Any Ice Today.

"It is simple. If a blind man plays an accordion on the street to make people cry it makes them sad and when they are sad the gold goes away off the accordion. And if a blind man goes to sleep because his music is full of sleepy songs like the long wind in a sleepy valley, then while the blind man is sleeping the diamonds in the diamond rabbit all go away. I play a sleepy song and go to sleep and I wake up and the diamond ear of the diamond rabbit is gone. I play another sleepy song and go to sleep and wake up and the diamond tail of the diamond rabbit is gone. After a while all the diamond rabbits are gone, even the diamond chin sitting on the diamond toenails of the rabbits next to the handles of the accordion, even those are gone."

"Is there anything I can do?" asked Any Ice Today.

"I do it myself," said the Potato Face Blind Man. "If I am too sorry I just play the sleepy song of the long wind going up the sleepy valleys. And that carries me away where I have time and money to dream about the new wonderful accordions and post offices where everybody that gets a letter and everybody that don't get a letter stops and remembers the Potato Face Blind Man."

How the Potato Face Blind Man Enjoyed Himself on a Fine Spring Morning

O N a Friday morning when the flummywisters were yodeling yisters high in the elm trees, the Potato Face Blind Man came down to his work sitting at the corner nearest the post office in the Village of Liver-and-

Onions and playing his gold-that-used-to-be accordion for the pleasure of the ears of the people going into the post office to see if they got any letters for themselves or their families.

"It is a good day, a lucky day," said the Potato Face Blind Man, "because for a beginning I have heard high in the elm trees the flummywisters yodeling their yisters in the long branches of the lingering leaves. So—so—I am going to listen to myself playing on my accordion the same yisters, the same yodels, drawing them like long glad breathings out of my glad accordion, long breathings of the branches of the lingering leaves."

And he sat down in his chair. On the sleeve of his coat he tied a sign, "I Am Blind *Too*." On the top button of his coat he hung a little thimble. On the bottom button of his coat he hung a tin copper cup. On the middle button he hung a wooden mug. By the side of him on the left side on the sidewalk he put a galvanized iron washtub, and on the right side an aluminum dishpan.

"It is a good day, a lucky day, and I am sure many people will stop and remember the Potato Face Blind Man," he sang to himself like a little song as he began running his fingers up and down the keys of the accordion like the yisters of the lingering leaves in the elm trees.

Then came Pick Ups. Always it happened Pick Ups asked questions and wished to know. And so this is how the questions and answers ran when the Potato Face filled the ears of Pick Ups with explanations.

"What is the piece you are playing on the keys of your accordion so fast sometimes, so slow sometimes, so sad

"I am sure many people will stop and remember the Potato Face Blind Man."

some of the moments, so glad some of the moments?"

"It is the song the mama flummywisters sing when they button loose the winter underwear of the baby flummywisters and sing:

'Fly, you little flummies,
Sing, you little wisters.' "

"And why do you have a little thimble on the top button of your coat?"

"That is for the dimes to be put in. Some people see it and say, 'Oh, I must put in a whole thimbleful of dimes.' "

"And the tin copper cup?"

"That is for the baseball players to stand off ten feet and throw in nickels and pennies. The one who throws the most into the cup will be the most lucky."

"And the wooden mug?"

"There is a hole in the bottom of it.

The hole is as big as the bottom. The nickel goes in and comes out again. It is for the very poor people who wish to give me a nickel and yet get the nickel back."

"The aluminum dishpan and the galvanized iron washtub—what are they doing by the side of you on both sides on the sidewalk?"

"Sometime maybe it will happen everybody who goes into the post office and comes out will stop and pour out all their money, because they might get afraid their money is no good any more. If such a happening ever happens then it will be nice for the people to have some place to pour their money. Such is the explanation why you see the aluminum dishpan and galvanized iron tub."

"Explain your sign—why is it, 'I Am Blind *Too*.' "

"Oh, I am sorry to explain to you, Pick Ups, why this is so which. Some of the people who pass by here going into the post office and coming out, they have eyes—but they see nothing with their eyes. They look where they are going and they get where they wish to get, but they forget why they came and they do not know how to come away. They are my blind brothers. It is for them I have the sign that reads, 'I Am Blind *Too*.' "

"I have my ears full of explanations and I thank you," said Pick Ups.

"Good-by," said the Potato Face Blind Man as he began drawing long breathings like lingering leaves out of the accordion—along with the song the mama flummywisters sing when they button loose the winter underwear of the baby flummywisters.

How Gimme the Ax Found Out About the Zigzag Railroad and Who Made It Zigzag

ONE day Gimme the Ax said to himself, "Today I go to the post office and around, looking around. Maybe I will hear about something happening last night when I was sleeping. Maybe a policeman began laughing and fell in a cistern and came out with a wheelbarrow full of goldfish wearing new jewelry. How do I know? Maybe the man in the moon going down a cellar stairs to get a pitcher of buttermilk for the woman in the moon to drink and stop crying, maybe he fell down the stairs and broke the pitcher and laughed and picked up the broken pieces and said to himself, 'One, two, three, four, accidents happen in the best regulated families.' How do I know?"

So with his mind full of simple and refreshing thoughts, Gimme the Ax went out into the backyard garden and looked at the different necktie poppies growing early in the summer. Then he picked one of the necktie poppies to wear for a necktie scarf going downtown to the post office and around looking around.

"It is a good speculation to look nice around looking around in a necktie scarf," said Gimme the Ax. "It is a necktie with a picture like whiteface pony spots on a green frog swimming in the moonshine."

So he went downtown. For the first time he saw the Potato Face Blind Man playing an accordion on the corner next nearest the post office. He asked the Potato Face to tell him why the railroad tracks run zigzag in the Rootabaga Country.

"Long ago," said the Potato Face Blind Man, "long before the necktie poppies began growing in the backyard, long before there was a necktie scarf like yours with whiteface pony spots on a green frog swimming in the moonshine, back in the old days when they laid the rails for the railroad they laid the rails straight.

"Then the zizzies came. The zizzy is a bug. He runs zigzag on zigzag legs, eats zigzag with zigzag teeth, and spits zigzag with a zigzag tongue.

"Millions of zizzies came hizzing with little hizzers on their heads and under their legs. They jumped on the rails with their zigzag legs, and spit and twisted with their zigzag teeth and tongues till they twisted the whole railroad and all the rails and tracks into a zigzag railroad with zigzag rails for the trains, the passenger trains and the freight trains, all to run zigzag on.

"Then the zizzies crept away into the fields where they sleep and cover themselves with zigzag blankets on special zigzag beds.

"Next day came shovelmen with their shovels, smooth engineers with smooth blue prints, and water boys with water pails and water dippers for the shovelmen to drink after shoveling the railroad straight. And I nearly forgot to say the steam and hoist operating engineers came and began their steam hoist and operating to make the railroad straight.

"They worked hard. They made the railroad straight again. They looked at the job and said to themselves and to each other, 'This is it—we done it.'

"Next morning the zizzies opened their zigzag eyes and looked over to the railroad and the rails. When they saw the railroad all straight again, and the rails and the ties and the spikes all straight again, the zizzies didn't even eat breakfast that morning.

"They jumped out of their zigzag beds, jumped onto the rails with their zigzag legs and spit and twisted till they spit and twisted all the rails and the ties and the spikes back into a zigzag like the letter Z and the letter Z at the end of the alphabet.

"After that the zizzies went to breakfast. And they said to themselves and to each other, the same as the shovelmen, the smooth engineers and the steam hoist and operating engineers, 'This is it—we done it.'"

"So that is the how of the which—it was the zizzies," said Gimme the Ax.

"Yes, it was the zizzies," said the Potato Face Blind Man. "That is the story told to me."

"Who told it to you?"

"*Two little zizzies.* They came to me one cold winter night and slept in my accordion where the music keeps it warm in winter. In the morning I said, 'Good morning, zizzies, did you have a good sleep last night and pleasant dreams?' And after they had breakfast they told me the story. Both told it zig-zag but it was the same kind of zigzag each had together."

The Story of Blixie Bimber and the Power of the Gold Buckskin Whincher

BLIXIE Bimber grew up looking for luck. If she found a horseshoe she took it home and put it on the wall of her room with a ribbon tied to it. She would look at the moon through her fingers, under her arms, over her right shoulder but never—never over her *left* shoulder. She listened and picked up everything anybody said about the groundhog and whether the groundhog saw his shadow when he came out the second of February.

If she dreamed of onions she knew the next day she would find a silver spoon. If she dreamed of fishes she knew the next day she would meet a strange man who would call her by her first name. She grew up looking for luck.

She was sixteen years old and quite a girl, with her skirts down to her shoe tops, when something happened. She was going to the post office to see if there was a letter for her from Peter Potato Blossom Wishes, her best chum, or a letter from Jimmy the Flea, her best friend she kept steady company with.

Jimmy the Flea was a climber. He

climbed skyscrapers and flagpoles and smokestacks and was a famous steeple-jack. Blixie Bimber liked him because he was a steeplejack, a little, but more because he was a whistler.

Every time Blixie said to Jimmy, "I got the blues—whistle the blues out of me," Jimmy would just naturally whistle till the blues just naturally went away from Blixie.

On the way to the post office, Blixie found a gold buckskin *whincher*. There it lay in the middle of the sidewalk. How and why it came to be there she never knew and nobody ever told her. "It's luck," she said to herself as she picked it up quick.

And so—she took it home and fixed it on a little chain and wore it around her neck.

She did not know and nobody ever told her a gold buckskin whincher is different from just a plain common whincher. It has a *power*. And if a thing has a power over you then you just naturally can't help yourself.

So—around her neck fixed on a little chain Blixie Bimber wore the gold buckskin whincher and never knew it had a power and all the time the power was working.

"The first man you meet with an X in his name you must fall head over heels in love with him," said the silent power in the gold buckskin whincher.

And that was why Blixie Bimber stopped at the post office and went back again asking the clerk at the post office window if he was sure there wasn't a letter for her. The name of the clerk was Silas Baxby. For six weeks he kept steady company with Blixie Bimber. They went to dances, hayrack rides, picnics, and high jinks together.

All the time the power in the gold buckskin whincher was working. It was hanging by a little chain around her neck and always working. It was saying, "The next man you meet with two X's in his name you must leave all and fall head over heels in love with him."

She met the high school principal. His name was Fritz Axenbax. Blixie dropped her eyes before him and threw smiles at him. And for six weeks he kept steady company with Blixie Bimber. They went to dances, hayrack rides, picnics, and high jinks together.

"Why do you go with him for steady company?" her relatives asked.

"It's a power he's got," Blixie answered, "I just can't help it—it's a power."

"One of his feet is bigger than the

other—how can you keep steady company with him?" they asked again.

All she would answer was, "It's a power."

All the time, of course, the gold buckskin whincher on the little chain around her neck was working. It was saying, "If she meets a man with three X's in his name she must fall head over heels in love with him."

At a band concert in the public square one night she met James Sixbixdix. There was no helping it. She dropped her eyes and threw her smiles at him. And for six weeks they kept steady company going to band concerts, dances, hayrack rides, picnics, and high jinks together.

"Why do you keep steady company with him? He's a musical soup eater," her relatives said to her. And she answered, "It's a power—I can't help myself."

Leaning down with her head in a rain water cistern one day, listening to the echoes against the strange wooden walls of the cistern, the gold buckskin whincher on the little chain around her neck slipped off and fell down into the rain water.

"My luck is gone," said Blixie. Then she went into the house and made two telephone calls. One was to James Sixbixdix telling him she couldn't keep the date with him that night. The other was to Jimmy the Flea, the climber, the steeplejack.

"Come on over—I got the blues and I want you to whistle 'em away," was what she telephoned Jimmy the Flea.

And so—if you ever come across a gold buckskin whincher, be careful.

It's got a power. It'll make you fall head over heels in love with the next man you meet with an X in his name. Or it will do other strange things because different whinchers have different powers.

*The Wedding Procession of
the Rag Doll and the
Broom Handle and
Who Was in It*

THE Rag Doll had many friends. The Whisk Broom, the Furnace Shovel, the Coffee Pot, they all liked the Rag Doll very much.

But, when the Rag Doll married, it was the Broom Handle she picked because the Broom Handle fixed her eyes.

A proud child, proud but careless, banged the head of the Rag Doll against a door one day and knocked off both the glass eyes sewed on long ago. It was then the Broom Handle found two black California prunes, and fastened the two California prunes just where the eyes belonged. So then the Rag Doll had two fine black eyes brand new. She was even nicknamed Black Eyes by some people.

There was a wedding when the Rag Doll married the Broom Handle. It was a grand wedding with one of the grandest processions ever seen at a rag doll wedding. And we are sure no broom handle ever had a grander wedding procession when he got married.

Who marched in the procession?
Well, first came the Spoon Lickers.
Every one of them had a tea spoon, or
a soup spoon, though most of them
had a big table spoon. On the spoons,
what did they have? Oh, some had
butter scotch, some had gravy, some
had marshmallow fudge. Every one
had something slickery sweet or fat to
eat on the spoon. And as they marched
in the wedding procession of the Rag
Doll and the Broom Handle, they
licked their spoons and looked around
and licked their spoons again.

Next came the Tin Pan Bangers.
Some had dishpans, some had frying
pans, some had potato peeling pans. All
the pans were tin with tight tin bottoms. And the Tin Pan Bangers
banged with knives and forks and iron
and wooden bangers on the bottoms of
the tin pans. And as they marched in

the wedding procession of the Rag Doll and the Broom Handle they banged their pans and looked around and banged again.

Then came the Chocolate Chins. They were all eating chocolates. And the chocolate was slippery and slickered all over their chins. Some of them spattered the ends of their noses with black chocolate. Some of them spread the brown chocolate nearly up to their ears. And then as they marched in the wedding procession of the Rag Doll and the Broom Handle they stuck their chins in the air and looked around and stuck their chins in the air again.

Then came the Dirty Bibs. They wore plain white bibs, checker bibs, stripe bibs, blue bibs, and bibs with butterflies. But all the bibs were dirty. The plain white bibs were dirty, the checker bibs were dirty, the stripe bibs,

the blue bibs, and the bibs with butterflies on them, they were all dirty. And
so in the wedding procession of the
Rag Doll and the Broom Handle the
Dirty Bibs marched with their dirty
fingers on the bibs and they looked
around and laughed and looked
around and laughed again.

Next came the Clean Ears. They
were proud. How they got into the
procession nobody knows. Their ears
were all clean. They were clean not
only on the outside but they were
clean on the inside. There was not a
speck of dirt or dust or muss or mess
on the inside nor the outside of their
ears. And so in the wedding procession
of the Rag Doll and the Broom Handle, they wiggled their ears and looked
around and wiggled their ears again.

The Easy Ticklers were next in the
procession. Their faces were shining.

Their cheeks were like bars of new soap. Their ribs were strong and the meat and the fat was thick on their ribs. It was plain to see they were saying, "Don't tickle me because I tickle so easy." And as they marched in the wedding procession of the Rag Doll and the Broom Handle, they tickled themselves and laughed and looked around and tickled themselves again.

The music was furnished mostly by the Musical Soup Eaters. They marched with big bowls of soup in front of them and big spoons for eating the soup. They whistled and chuzzled and snozzled the soup and the noise they made could be heard far up at the head of the procession where the Spoon Lickers were marching. So they dipped their soup and looked around and dipped their soup again.

The Chubby Chubs were next.

They were roly poly, round faced smackers and snoozers. They were not fat babies—oh no, oh no—not fat but just chubby and easy to squeeze. They marched on their chubby legs and chubby feet and chubbed their chubbs and looked around and chubbed their chubbs again.

The last of all in the wedding procession of the Rag Doll and the Broom Handle were the Sleepyheads. They were smiling and glad to be marching but their heads were slimpsing down and their smiles were half fading away and their eyes were half shut or a little more than half shut. They staggered just a little as though their feet were not sure where they were going. They were the Sleepyheads, the last of all, in the wedding procession of the Rag Doll and the Broom Handle and the

Sleepyheads they never looked around at all.

It *was* a grand procession, don't you think so?

How the Hat Ashes Shovel
Helped Snoo Foo

IF you want to remember the names of all six of the Sniggers children, remember that the three biggest were named Blink, Swink, and Jink but the three littlest ones were named Blunk, Swunk, and Junk. One day last January the three biggest had a fuss with the three littlest. The fuss was about a new hat for Snoo Foo, the snow man, about what kind of a hat he should wear and how he should wear it. Blink, Swink, and Jink said, "He wants a crooked hat put on straight." Blunk, Swunk, and Junk said, "He wants a straight hat put on crooked." They fussed and fussed. Blink fussed with Blunk, Swink fussed with Swunk, and Jink fussed with Junk. The first ones to make up after the fuss were Jink and Junk. They decided the best way to settle the fuss. "Let's put a crooked hat on crooked," said Jink. "No, let's put a straight hat on straight," said Junk. Then they stood looking and looking into each other's shiny laughing eyes and then both of them exploded to each other at the same time, "Let's put on two hats, a crooked hat crooked and a straight hat straight.''

Well, they looked around for hats. But there were not any hats anywhere, that is, no hats big enough for a snow man with a big head like Snoo Foo. So they went in the house and asked their mother for *the hat ashes shovel*. Of course, in most any other house, the mother would be all worried if six children came tramping and clomping in, banging the door, and all six ejaculating to their mother at once, ''Where is the hat ashes shovel?'' But Missus Sniggers wasn't worried at all. She rubbed her chin with her finger and said softly, ''Oh lah de dah, oh lah de dah, where is that hat ashes shovel, last week I had it when I was making a hat for Mister Sniggers; I remember I had that hat ashes shovel right up here over the clock, oh lah de dah, oh lah de dah.

Go out and ring the front door bell," she said to Jink Sniggers. Jink ran away to the front door. And Missus Sniggers and the five children waited. Bling-bling the bell began ringing and—listen—the door of the clock opened and the hat ashes shovel fell out. "Oh lah de dah, get out of here in a hurry," said Missus Sniggers.

Well, the children ran out and dug a big pail of hat ashes with the hat ashes shovel. And they made two hats for Snoo Foo. One was a crooked hat. The other was a straight hat. And they put the crooked hat on crooked and the straight hat on straight. And there stood Snoo Foo in the front yard and everybody who came by on the street, he would take off his hat to them, the crooked hat with his arm crooked and the straight hat with his arm straight. That was the end of the fuss between the Sniggers children and it was Jink, the littlest one of the biggest, and Junk, the littlest one of the littlest, who settled the fuss by looking clean into each other's eyes and laughing. If you ever get into a fuss try this way of settling it.

How Bimbo the Snip's Thumb Stuck to His Nose When the Wind Changed

ONCE there was a boy in the Village of Liver-and-Onions whose name was Bimbo the Snip. He forgot nearly everything his father and mother told him to do and told him not to do.

One day his father, Bevo the Hike, came home and found Bimbo the Snip sitting on the front steps with his thumb fastened to his nose and the fingers wiggling.

"I can't take my thumb away," said Bimbo the Snip, "because when I put my thumb to my nose and wiggled my fingers at the iceman the wind changed. And just like mother always said, if the wind changed the thumb would stay fastened to my nose and not come off."

Bevo the Hike took hold of the thumb and pulled. He tied a clothes line rope around it and pulled. He pushed with his foot and heel against it. And all the time the thumb stuck fast and the fingers wiggled from the end of the nose of Bimbo the Snip.

Bevo the Hike sent for the ward alderman. The ward alderman sent for the barn boss of the street cleaning department. The barn boss of the street cleaning department sent for the head vaccinator of the vaccination bureau of the health department. The head vaccinator of the vaccination bureau of the health department sent for the big main fixer of the weather bureau where they understand the tricks of the wind and the wind changing.

And the big main fixer of the weather bureau said, "If you hit the thumb six times with the end of a traffic policeman's club, the thumb will come loose."

So Bevo the Hike went to a traffic policeman standing on a street corner with a whistle telling the wagons and cars which way to go.

He told the traffic policeman, "The wind changed and Bimbo the Snip's thumb is fastened to his nose and will not come loose till it is hit six times with the end of a traffic policeman's club."

"I can't help you unless you find a monkey to take my place standing on the corner telling the wagons and cars which way to go," answered the traffic policeman.

So Bevo the Hike went to the zoo and said to a monkey, "The wind changed and Bimbo the Snip's thumb is fastened to his nose and will not come loose till it is hit with the end of a traffic policeman's club six times and the traffic policeman cannot leave his place on the street corner telling the traffic which way to go unless a monkey comes and takes his place."

The monkey answered, "Get me a ladder with a whistle so I can climb up and whistle and tell the traffic which way to go."

So Bevo the Hike hunted and hunted over the city and looked and looked and asked and asked till his feet and his eyes and his head and his heart were tired from top to bottom.

Then he met an old widow woman whose husband had been killed in a sewer explosion when he was digging sewer ditches. And the old woman was carrying a bundle of picked-up kindling wood in a bag on her back because she did not have money enough to buy coal.

Bevo the Hike told her, "You have troubles. So have I. You are carrying a load on your back people can see. I am carrying a load and nobody sees it."

"Tell me your troubles," said the old widow woman. He told her. And she said, "In the next block is an old umbrella handle maker. He has a ladder with a whistle. He climbs on the ladder when he makes long long umbrella handles. And he has the whistle on the ladder to be whistling."

Bevo the Hike went to the next block, found the house of the umbrella handle maker and said to him, "The wind changed and Bimbo the Snip's thumb is fastened to his nose and will not come loose till it is hit with the end of a traffic policeman's club six times and the traffic policeman cannot leave the corner where he is telling the traffic which way to go unless a monkey takes his place and the monkey cannot take his place unless he has a ladder with a whistle to stand on and whistle the wagons and cars which way to go."

Then the umbrella handle maker said, "Tonight I have a special job because I must work on a long, long umbrella handle and I will need the ladder to climb up and the whistle to be whistling. But if you promise to have the ladder back by tonight you can take it."

Bevo the Hike promised. Then he took the ladder with a whistle to the monkey, the monkey took the place of the traffic policeman while the traffic policeman went to the home of Bevo the Hike where Bimbo the Snip was sitting on the front steps with his thumb fastened to his nose wiggling his fingers at everybody passing by on the street.

The traffic policeman hit Bimbo the Snip's thumb five times with the club. And the thumb stuck fast. But the sixth time it was hit with the end of the traffic policeman's thumb club, it came loose.

Then Bevo thanked the policeman, thanked the monkey, and took the lad-

The monkey took the place of the traffic policeman.

der with the whistle back to the umbrella handle maker's house and thanked him.

When Bevo the Hike got home that night Bimbo the Snip was in bed and all tickled. He said to his father, "I will be careful how I stick my thumb to my nose and wiggle my fingers the next time the wind changes."

The Two Skyscrapers Who Decided to Have a Child

T W O skyscrapers stood across the street from each other in the Village of Liver-and-Onions. In the daylight when the streets poured full of people buying and selling, these two skyscrapers talked with each other the same as mountains talk.

In the night time when all the people buying and selling were gone home and there were only policemen and taxicab drivers on the streets, in the night when a mist crept up the streets and threw a purple and gray wrapper over everything, in the night when the stars and the sky shook out sheets of purple and gray mist down over the town, then the two skyscrapers leaned toward each other and whispered.

Whether they whispered secrets to each other or whether they whispered simple things that you and I know and everybody knows, that is their secret. One thing is sure: they often were seen leaning toward each other and whispering in the night the same as mountains lean and whisper in the night.

High on the roof of one of the skyscrapers was a tin brass goat looking out across prairies, and silver blue lakes shining like blue porcelain breakfast plates, and out across silver snakes of winding rivers in the morning sun. And high on the roof of the other sky-scraper was a tin brass goose looking out across prairies, and silver blue lakes shining like blue porcelain breakfast plates, and out across silver snakes of winding rivers in the morning sun.

Now the Northwest Wind was a friend of the two skyscrapers. Coming so far, coming five hundred miles in a few hours, coming so fast always while the skyscrapers were standing still, standing always on the same old street corners always, the Northwest Wind was a bringer of news.

"Well, I see the city is here yet," the Northwest Wind would whistle to the skyscrapers.

And they would answer, "Yes, and

are the mountains standing yet way out yonder where you come from, Wind?"

"Yes, the mountains are there yonder, and farther yonder is the sea, and the railroads are still going, still running across the prairie to the mountains, to the sea," the Northwest Wind would answer.

And now there was a pledge made by the Northwest Wind to the two skyscrapers. Often the Northwest Wind shook the tin brass goat and shook the tin brass goose on top of the skyscrapers.

"Are you going to blow loose the tin brass goat on my roof?" one asked.

"Are you going to blow loose the tin brass goose on my roof?" the other asked.

"Oh, no," the Northwest Wind laughed, first to one and then to the other, "if I ever blow loose your tin brass goat and if I ever blow loose your tin brass goose, it will be when I am sorry for you because you are up against hard luck and there is somebody's funeral."

So time passed on and the two skyscrapers stood with their feet among the policemen and the taxicabs, the people buying and selling,—the customers with parcels, packages, and bundles—while away high on their roofs stood the goat and the goose looking out on silver blue lakes like blue porcelain breakfast plates and silver snakes of rivers winding in the morning sun.

So time passed on and the Northwest Wind kept coming, telling the news and making promises.

So time passed on. And the two skyscrapers decided to have a child.

And they decided when their child came it should be a *free* child.

"It must be a free child," they said to each other. "It must not be a child standing still all its life on a street corner. Yes, if we have a child she must be free to run across the prairie, to the mountains, to the sea. Yes, it must be a free child."

So time passed on. Their child came. It was a railroad train, the Golden Spike Limited, the fastest long distance train in the Rootabaga Country. It ran across the prairie, to the mountains, to the sea.

They were glad, the two skyscrapers were, glad to have a free child running away from the big city, far away to the mountains, far away to the sea, running as far as the farthest mountains and sea coasts touched by the Northwest Wind.

They were glad their child was useful, the two skyscrapers were, glad their child was carrying a thousand people a thousand miles a day, so when people spoke of the Golden Spike Limited, they spoke of it as a strong, lovely child.

Then time passed on. There came a day when the newsies yelled as though they were crazy. "Yah yah, blah blah, yoh yoh," was what it sounded like to the two skyscrapers who never bothered much about what the newsies were yelling.

"Yah yah, blah blah, yoh yoh," was the cry of the newsies that came up again to the tops of the skyscrapers.

At last the yelling of the newsies came so strong the skyscrapers listened and heard the newsies yammering, "All about the great train wreck! All about the Golden Spike disaster! Many lives lost! Many lives lost!''

And the Northwest Wind came howling a slow sad song. And late that afternoon a crowd of policemen, taxi-cab drivers, newsies, and customers with bundles, all stood around talking and wondering about two things next to each other on the street car track in the middle of the street. One was a tin brass goat. The other was a tin brass goose. And they lay next to each other.

The White Horse Girl and the Blue Wind Boy

W HEN the dishes are washed at night time and the cool of the evening has come in summer or the lamps and fires are lit for the night in winter, then the fathers and mothers in the Rootabaga Country sometimes tell the young people the story of the

White Horse Girl and the Blue Wind Boy.

The White Horse Girl grew up far in the west of the Rootabaga Country. All the years she grew up as a girl she liked to ride horses. Best of all things for her was to be straddle of a white horse loping with a loose bridle among the hills and along the rivers of the west Rootabaga Country.

She rode one horse white as snow, another horse white as new washed sheep wool, and another white as silver. And she could not tell because she did not know which of these three white horses she liked best.

"Snow is beautiful enough for me any time," she said, "new washed sheep wool, or silver out of a ribbon of the new moon, any or either is white enough for me. I like the white manes, the white flanks, the white noses, the white feet of all my ponies. I like the forelocks hanging down between the white ears of all three—my ponies."

And living neighbor to the White Horse Girl in the same prairie country, with the same black crows flying over their places, was the Blue Wind Boy. All the years he grew up as a boy he liked to walk with his feet in the dirt and the grass listening to the winds. Best of all things for him was to put on strong shoes and go hiking among the hills and along the rivers of the west Rootabaga Country, listening to the winds.

There was a blue wind of day time, starting sometimes six o'clock on a summer morning or eight o'clock on a winter morning. And there was a night wind with blue of summer stars in summer and blue of winter stars in winter. And there was yet another, a blue wind of the times between night and day, a blue dawn and evening wind. All three of these winds he liked so well he could not say which he liked best.

"The early morning wind is strong as the prairie and whatever I tell it I know it believes and remembers," he said, "and the night wind with the big dark curves of the night sky in it, the night wind gets inside of me and understands all my secrets. And the blue wind of the times between, in the dusk when it is neither night nor day, this is the wind that asks me questions and tells me to wait and it will bring me whatever I want."

Of course, it happened as it had to happen, the White Horse Girl and the Blue Wind Boy met. She, straddling one of her white horses, and he, wearing his strong hiking shoes in the dirt and the grass, it had to happen they should meet among the hills and along the rivers of the west Rootabaga Country where they lived neighbors.

And of course, she told him all about the snow white horse and the horse white as new washed sheep wool and the horse white as a silver ribbon of the new moon. And he told her all about the blue winds he liked listening to, the early morning wind, the night sky wind, and the wind of the dusk between, the wind that asked him questions and told him to wait.

One day the two of them were gone. On the same day of the week the White Horse Girl and the Blue Wind Boy went away. And their fathers and mothers and sisters and brothers and uncles and aunts wondered about them and talked about them, because they didn't tell anybody beforehand they were going. Nobody at all knew beforehand or afterward why they were going away, the real honest why of it.

They left a short letter. It read:

To All Our Sweethearts, Old Folks and Young Folks:

We have started to go where the white horses come from and where the blue winds begin. Keep a corner in your hearts for us while we are gone.

The White Horse Girl.
The Blue Wind Boy.

That was all they had to guess by in the west Rootabaga Country, to guess and guess where two darlings had gone.

Many years passed. One day there came riding across the Rootabaga Country a Gray Man on Horseback.

He looked like he had come a long ways. So they asked him the question they always asked of any rider who looked like he had come a long ways, "Did you ever see the White Horse Girl and the Blue Wind Boy?"

"Yes," he answered, "I saw them.

"It was a long, long ways from here I saw them," he went on, "it would take years and years to ride to where they are. They were sitting together and talking to each other, sometimes singing, in a place where the land runs high and tough rocks reach up. And they were looking out across water, blue water as far as the eye could see. And away far off the blue waters met the blue sky.

" 'Look!' said the Boy, 'that's where the blue winds begin.'

"And far out on the blue waters, just a little this side of where the blue winds begin, there were white manes, white flanks, white noses, white galloping feet.

"'Look!' said the Girl, 'that's where the white horses come from.'

"And then nearer to the land came thousands in an hour, millions in a day, white horses, some white as snow, some like new washed sheep wool, some white as silver ribbons of the new moon.

"I asked them, 'Whose place is this?' They answered, 'It belongs to us; this is what we started for; this is where the white horses come from; this is where the blue winds begin.'"

And that was all the Gray Man on Horseback would tell the people of the west Rootagaba Country. That was all he knew, he said, and if there was any more he would tell it.

And the fathers and mothers and sisters and brothers and uncles and aunts of the White Horse Girl and the Blue Wind Boy wondered and talked often about whether the Gray Man on Horseback made up the story out of his head or whether it happened just like he told it.

Anyhow this is the story they tell sometimes to the young people of the west Rootabaga Country when the dishes are washed at night and the cool of the evening has come in summer or the lamps and fires are lit for the night in winter.

How to Tell Corn Fairies If You See 'Em

I F you have ever watched the little corn begin to march across the black lands and then slowly change to big corn and go marching on from the little corn moon of summer to the big corn harvest moon of autumn, then you must have guessed who it is that helps the corn come along. It is the corn fairies. Leave out the corn fairies and there wouldn't be any corn.

All children know this. All boys and girls know that corn is no good unless there are corn fairies.

Have you ever stood in Illinois or Iowa and watched the late summer wind or the early fall wind running across a big cornfield? It looks as if a big, long blanket were being spread out for dancers to come and dance on. If you look close and if you listen close you can see the corn fairies come dancing and singing—sometimes. If it is a wild day and a hot sun is pouring down while a cool north wind blows—and this happens sometimes— then you will be sure to see thousands of corn fairies marching and counter-marching in mocking grand marches over the big, long blanket of green and silver. Then too they sing, only you must listen with your littlest and newest ears if you wish to hear their singing. They sing soft songs that go pla-sizzy pla-sizzy-sizzy, and each song is softer than an eye wink, softer than a Nebraska baby's thumb.

And Spink, who is a little girl living in the same house with the man writing this story, and Skabootch, who is another little girl in the same house— both Spink and Skabootch are asking the question, "How can we tell corn fairies if we see 'em? If we meet a corn fairy how will we know it?" And this is the explanation the man gave to Spink who is older than Skabootch, and to Skabootch who is younger than Spink:

All corn fairies wear overalls. They work hard, the corn fairies, and they are proud. The reason they are proud is because they work so hard. And the reason they work so hard is because they have overalls.

But understand this. The overalls are corn gold cloth, woven from leaves of ripe corn mixed with ripe October corn silk. In the first week of the harvest moon coming up red and changing to yellow and silver the corn fairies sit by thousands between the corn rows weaving and stitching the clothes they have to wear next winter, next spring, next summer.

They sit cross-legged when they sew. And it is a law among them each one must point the big toe at the moon while sewing the harvest moon clothes. When the moon comes up red as blood early in the evening they point their big toes slanting toward the east. Then toward midnight when the moon is yellow and half way up the sky their big toes are only half slanted as they sit cross-legged sewing. And after midnight when the moon sails its silver disk high overhead and toward the west, then the corn fairies sit sewing with their big toes pointed nearly straight up.

If it is a cool night and looks like frost, then the laughter of the corn fairies is something worth seeing. All the time they sit sewing their next year clothes they are laughing. It is not a law they have to laugh. They laugh because they are half-tickled and glad because it is a good corn year.

And whenever the corn fairies laugh then the laugh comes out of the mouth like a thin gold frost. If you should be lucky enough to see a thousand corn fairies sitting between the corn rows and all of them laughing, you would laugh with wonder yourself to see the gold frost coming from their mouths while they laughed.

Travelers who have traveled far, and seen many things, say that if you know the corn fairies with a real knowledge you can always tell by the stitches in their clothes what state they are from.

In Illinois the corn fairies stitch fifteen stitches of ripe corn silk across the woven corn leaf cloth. In Iowa they stitch sixteen stitches, in Nebraska seventeen, and the farther west you go the more corn silk stitches the corn fairies have in the corn cloth clothes they wear.

In Minnesota one year there were fairies with a blue sash of corn-flowers across the breast. In the Dakotas the same year all the fairies wore pumpkin-flower neckties, yellow four-in-hands and yellow ascots. And in one strange year it happened in both the states of Ohio and Texas the corn fairies wore little wristlets of white morning glories.

The traveler who heard about this asked many questions and found out the reason why that year the corn fairies wore little wristlets of white morning glories. He said, "Whenever fairies are sad they wear white. And this year, which was long ago, was the year men were tearing down all the old zigzag rail fences. Now those old zigzag rail fences were beautiful for the fairies because a hundred fairies could sit on one rail and thousands and thousands of them could sit on the zigzags and sing pla-sizzy pla-sizzy, softer than an eye wink, softer than a baby's thumb, all on a moonlight summer night. And they found out that year was going to be the last year of the zigzag rail fences. It made them sorry and sad, and when they are sorry and sad they wear white. So they picked the wonderful white morning glories running along the zig-zag rail fences and made them into little wristlets and wore those wristlets the next year to show they were sorry and sad."

Of course, all this helps you to know how the corn fairies look in the evening, the night time, and the moonlight. Now we shall see how they look in the day time.

In the day time the corn fairies have their overalls of corn gold cloth on. And they walk among the corn rows and climb the corn stalks and fix things in the leaves and stalks and ears of the corn. They help it to grow.

Each one carries on the left shoulder a mouse brush to brush away the field mice. And over the right shoulder each one has a cricket broom to sweep away the crickets. The brush is a whisk brush to brush away mice that get foolish. And the broom is to sweep away crickets that get foolish.

Around the middle of each corn fairy is a yellow-belly belt. And stuck in this belt is a purple moon shaft hammer. Whenever the wind blows strong and nearly blows the corn down, then the fairies run out and take their purple moon shaft hammers out of their yellow-belly belts and nail down nails to keep the corn from blowing down. When a rain storm is blowing up terrible and driving all kinds of terribles across the cornfield, then you can be sure of one thing. Running like the wind among the corn rows are the fairies, jerking their purple moon shaft hammers out of their belts and nailing nails down to keep the corn standing up so it will grow and be ripe and beautiful when the harvest moon comes again in the fall.

Spink and Skabootch ask where the corn fairies get the nails. The answer to Spink and Skabootch is, "Next week you will learn all about where the corn fairies get the nails to nail down the corn if you will keep your faces washed and your ears washed till next week."

And the next time you stand watching a big cornfield in late summer or early fall, when the wind is running across the green and silver, listen with your littlest and newest ears. Maybe you will hear the corn fairies going pla-sizzy pla-sizzy-sizzy, softer than an eye wink, softer than a Nebraska baby's thumb.

How Six Pigeons Came Back to Hatrack the Horse After Many Accidents and Six Telegrams

S IX crooked ladders stood against the front of the shanty where Hatrack the Horse lived.

Yellow roses all on fire were climbing up and down the ladders, up and down and crossways.

And leaning out on both sides from the crooked ladders were vines of yellow roses, leaning, curving, nearly falling.

Hatrack the Horse was waiting. This was the morning Wiffle the Chick was coming.

"Sit here on the cracker box and listen," he said to her when she came, "listen and you will hear the roses saying, 'This is climbing time for all yellow roses and climbing time is the time to climb; how did we ever learn to climb only by climbing?' Listen and you will hear—'st . . th . . st . . th . . st . . th . .' it is the feet of the yellow roses climbing up and down and leaning out and curving and nearly falling '. . st . . th . . st . . th . .' "

So Wiffle the Chick sat there, early in the summer, enjoying herself, sitting on a cracker box, listening to the yellow roses climb around the six crooked ladders.

Hatrack the Horse came out. On his shoulders were two pigeons, on his hands two pigeons. And he reached his hand around behind his back where his hat was hanging and he opened the hat and showed Wiffle the Chick two pigeons in the hat.

"They are lovely pigeons to look at and their eyes are full of lessons to learn," said Wiffle the Chick. "Maybe you will tell me why you have their feet wrapped in bandages, hospital liniment bandages full of hospital liniment smells? Why do you put soft mittens on the feet of these pigeons so lovely to look at?"

"They came back yesterday, they came back home," was the answer. "They came back limping on their feet with the toes turned in so far they nearly turned backward. When they put their bleeding feet in my hands one by one each one, it was like each one was writing his name in my hand with red ink."

"Did you know they were coming?" asked Wiffle.

"Every day the last six days I get a telegram, six telegrams from six pigeons—and at last they come home. And ever since they come home they are telling me they come because they love Hatrack the Horse and the yellow climbing roses climbing over the six crooked ladders."

"Did you name your pigeons with names?" asked Wiffle.

"These three, the sandy and golden brown, all named themselves by where they came from. This is Chickamauga, here is Chattanooga, and this is Chattahoochee. And the other three all got their names from me when I was feeling high and easy. This is Blue Mist, here is Bubbles, and last of all take a look at Wednesday Evening in the Twilight and the Gloaming."

"Do you always call her Wednesday Evening in the Twilight and the Gloaming?"

"Not when I am making coffee for breakfast. If I am making coffee for breakfast then I just call her Wednesday Evening."

"Didn't you tie the mittens on her feet extra special nice?"

"Yes—she is an extra special nice pigeon. She cries for pity when she wants pity. And she shuts her eyes when she doesn't want to look at you. And if you look deep in her eyes when her eyes are open you will see lights there exactly like the lights on the pastures and the meadows when the mist is drifting on a Wednesday evening just between the twilight and the gloaming.

"A week ago yesterday they all went away. And they won't tell why they went away. Somebody clipped their wings, cut off their flying feathers so they couldn't fly—and they won't tell why. They were six hundred miles from home—but they won't tell how they counted the six hundred miles. A hundred miles a day they walked, six hundred miles in a week, and they sent a telegram to me every day, one writing a telegram one day and another writing a telegram the next day—all the time walking a hundred miles a day with their toes turned in like pigeon toes turn in. Do you wonder they needed bandages, hospital liniment bandages on their feet—and soft mittens?"

"Show me the telegrams they sent you, one every day for six days while they were walking six hundred miles on their pigeon toes."

So Hatrack the Horse got the six telegrams. The reading on the telegrams was like this:

1. "Feet are as good as wings if you have to. CHICKAMAUGA."
2. "If you love to go somewhere it is easy to walk. CHATTANOOGA."
3. "In the night sleeping you forget whether you have wings or feet or neither. CHATTAHOOCHEE."
4. "What are toes for if they don't point to what you want? BLUE MIST."
5. "Anybody can walk hundreds of miles putting one foot ahead of the other. BUBBLES."
6. "Pity me. Far is far. Near is near. And there is no place like home when the yellow roses climb up

the ladders and sing in the early summer. Pity me. WEDNESDAY EVENING IN THE TWILIGHT AND THE GLOAMING."

"Did they have any accidents going six hundred miles walking with their little pigeon toes turned in?" asked Wiffle.

"Once they had an accident," said Hatrack, with Chattahoochee standing in his hat, Chickamauga on his right shoulder, Chattanooga on his left, and holding Blue Mist and Bubbles on his wrists. "They came to an old wooden bridge. Chattahoochee and Wednesday Evening both cried out, 'The bridge will fall if we all walk on it the same time!' But they were all six already on the bridge and the bridge began sagging and tumbled them all into the river. But it was good for them all to have a footbath for their feet, Wednesday Evening explained."

"I got a suspicion you like Wednesday Evening in the Twilight and the Gloaming best of all," spoke up Wiffle.

"Well, Wednesday Evening was the only one I noticed making any mention of the yellow roses in her telegram," Hatrack the Horse explained, as he picked up Wednesday Evening and reached her around and put her to perch on the shoulder bone on his back.

Then the old man and the girl sat on the cracker box saying nothing, only listening to the yellow roses all on fire with early summer climbing up the crooked ladders, up and down and crossways, some of them leaning out and curving and nearly falling.

How Johnny the Wham Sleeps in Money All the Time and Joe the Wimp Shines and Sees Things

ONCE the Potato Face Blind Man began talking about arithmetic and geography, where numbers come from and why we add and subtract before we multiply, when the first fractions and decimal points were invented, who gave the rivers their names, and why some rivers have short names slipping off the tongue easy as whistling, and why other rivers have long names wearing the stub ends off lead pencils.

The girl, Ax Me No Questions, asked the old man if boys always stay in the home towns where they are born and grow up, or whether boys pack their packsacks and go away somewhere else after they grow up. This question started the old man telling about Johnny the Wham and Joe the Wimp and things he remembered about them:

Johnny the Wham and Joe the Wimp are two boys who used to live here in the Village of Liver-and-Onions before they went away. They grew up here, carving their initials, J. W., on wishbones and peanuts and wheelbarrows. And if anybody found a wishbone or a peanut or a wheelbarrow with the initials, J. W., carved on it, he didn't know whether it was Johnny the Wham or Joe the Wimp.

They met on summer days, put their hands in their pockets, and traded each other grasshoppers learning to say yes and no. One kick and a spit meant yes. Two kicks and a spit meant no. One two three, four five six of a kick and a spit meant the grasshopper was counting and learning numbers.

They promised what they were going to do after they went away from the village. Johnny the Wham said, "I am going to sleep in money up to my knees with thousand dollar bills all over me for a blanket." Joe the Wimp said, "I am going to see things and shine, and I am going to shine and see things."

They went away. They did what they said. They went up into the grasshopper country near the Village of Eggs Over where the grasshoppers were eating the corn in the fields without counting how much. They stayed in those fields till those grasshoppers learned to say yes and no and learned to count. One kick and a spit meant yes. Two kicks and a spit meant no. One two three, four five six meant the grasshoppers were counting and learning numbers. The grasshoppers, after that, eating ears of corn in the fields, were counting how many and how much.

Today Johnny the Wham sleeps in a room full of money in the big bank in the Village of Eggs Over. The room where he sleeps is the room where they keep the thousand dollar bills. He walks in thousand dollar bills up to his knees at night before he goes to bed on the floor. A bundle of thousand dollar bills is his pillow. He covers himself like a man in a haystack or a strawstack, with thousand dollar bills. The paper money is piled around him in armfuls and sticks up and stands out around him the same as hay or straw.

And Lizzie Lazarus, who talked with him in the Village of Eggs Over last week, she says Johnny the Wham told her, "There is music in thousand dollar bills. Before I go to sleep at night and when I wake up in the morning, I listen to their music. They whisper and cry, they sing little oh-me, oh-my songs as they wriggle and rustle next to each other. A few with dirty faces, with torn ears, with patches and finger and thumb prints on their faces, they cry and whisper so it hurts to hear them. And often they shake all over, laughing.

"I heard one dirty thousand dollar bill say to another spotted with patches and thumb prints, 'They kiss us welcome when we come, they kiss us sweet good-by when we go.'

"They cry and whisper and laugh about things and special things and extra extra special things—pigeons, ponies, pigs, special pigeons, ponies, pigs, extra extra special pigeons, ponies, pigs—cats, pups, monkeys, big bags of cats, pups, monkeys, extra extra big bags of special cats, pups, monkeys—jewelry, ice cream, bananas, pie, hats, shoes, shirts, dust pans, rat traps, coffee cups, handkerchiefs, safety pins—diamonds, bottles, and big front doors with bells on—they cry and whisper and laugh about these things—and it never hurts unless the dirty thousand dollar bills with torn ears and patches on their faces say to each other, 'They kiss us welcome when we come, they kiss us sweet good-by when we go.' ''

The old Potato Face sat saying nothing. He fooled a little with the accordion keys as if trying to make up a tune for the words, "They kiss us welcome when we come, they kiss us sweet good-by when we go."

Ax Me No Questions looked at him with a soft look and said softly, "Now maybe you'll tell about Joe the Wimp." And he told her:

Joe the Wimp shines the doors in front of the bank. The doors are brass, and Joe the Wimp stands with rags and ashes and chamois skin keeping the brass shining.

"The brass shines slick and shows everything on the street like a looking glass," he told Lizzie Lazarus last week. "If pigeons, ponies, pigs, come past, or cats, pups, monkeys, or jewelry, ice cream, bananas, pie, hats, shoes, shirts, dust pans, rat traps, coffee cups, handkerchiefs, safety pins, or diamonds, bottles, and big front doors with bells on, Joe the Wimp sees them in the brass.

"I rub on the brass doors, and things begin to jump into my hands out of the shine of the brass. Faces, chimneys, elephants, yellow humming birds, and blue cornflowers, where I have seen grasshoppers sleeping two by two and two by two, they all come to the shine of the brass on the doors when I ask them to. If you shine brass hard, and wish as hard as the brass wishes, and keep on shining and wishing, then always things come jumping into your hands out of the shine of the brass."

"So you see," said the Potato Face Blind Man to Ax Me No Questions, "sometimes the promises boys make when they go away come true afterward."

"They got what they asked for—now will they keep it or leave it?" said Ax Me.

"Only the grasshoppers can answer that," was the old man's reply. "The grasshoppers are older. They know more about jumps. And especially grasshoppers that say yes and no and count one two three, four five six."

And he sat saying nothing, fooling with the accordion keys as if trying to make up a tune for the words, "They

kiss us welcome when we come, they
kiss us sweet good-by when we go."

How Deep Red Roses Goes Back and Forth between the Clock and the Looking Glass

ONE morning when big white clouds were shouldering each other's shoulders, rolling on the rollers of a big blue sky, Blixie Bimber came along where the Potato Face Blind Man sat shining the brass bickerjiggers on his accordion.

"Do you like to shine up the brass bickerjiggers?" asked Blixie.

"Yes," he answered. "One time a long time ago the brass bickerjiggers were gold, but they stole the gold away when I wasn't looking."

He blinked the eyelids over his eyeballs and said, "I thank them because they took gold they wanted. Brass feels good to my fingers the same as gold." And he went on shining up the brass bickerjiggers on the accordion, humming a little line of an old song, "Tomorrow will never catch up with yesterday because yesterday started sooner."

"Seems like a nice morning with the sun spilling bushels of sunshine," he said to Blixie, who answered, "Big white clouds are shouldering each other's shoulders rolling on the rollers of a big blue sky."

"Seems like it's April all over again," he murmured, almost like he wasn't talking at all.

"Seems just that way—April all over again," murmured Blixie, almost like she wasn't talking at all.

So they began drifting, the old man drifting his way, the girl drifting her way, till he drifted into a story. And the story he told was like this and in these words:

"Deep Red Roses was a lovely girl with blue skylights like the blue skylights of early April in her eyes. And her lips reminded people of deep red roses waiting in the cool of the summer evening.

"She met Shoulder Straps one day when she was young yet. He promised her. And she promised him. But he went away. One of the long wars between two short wars took him. In a far away country, then, he married another girl. And he didn't come back to Deep Red Roses.

"Next came High High Over, one day when she was young yet. A dancer he was, going from one city to another city to dance, spending his afternoons and evenings and late nights dancing, and sleeping in the morning till noon. And when he promised she promised. But he went away to another city and after that another city. And he married one woman and then another woman. Every year there came a new story about one of the new wives of High High Over, the dancer. And while she was young yet, Deep Red Roses forgot all about her promise and the promise of High High Over, the dancer who ran away from her.

"Six Bits was the next to come along. And he was not a soldier nor a dancer nor anything special. He was a careless man, changing from one job to another, changing from paperhanging to plastering, from fixing shingle roofs where the shingles were ripped to opening cans with can openers.

"Six Bits gave Deep Red Roses his promise and she gave him her promise. But he was always late keeping his promise. When the wedding was to be Tuesday he didn't come till Wednesday. If it was Friday he came Saturday. And there wasn't any wedding.

"So Deep Red Roses said to herself, 'I am going away and learn, I am going away and talk with the wives of High High Over, the dancer, and maybe if I go far enough I will find the wife of Shoulder Straps, the soldier—and maybe the wives of the men who promised me will tell me how to keep promises kept.'

"She packed her baggage till her baggage was packed so full there was room for only one more thing. So she had to decide whether to put a *clock* or whether to put a *looking glass* in her baggage.

" 'My head tells me to carry the clock so I can always tell if I am early or late,' she said to herself. 'But my heart tells me to carry a looking glass so I can look at my face and tell if I am getting older or younger.'

"At last she decides to take the clock and leave the looking glass—because her head says so. She starts away. She goes through the door, she is out of the house, she goes to the street, she starts up the street.

"Then her heart tells her to go back and change the clock for the looking glass. She goes back up the street, through the door, into the house, into her room. Now she stands in front of the clock and the looking glass saying, 'Tonight I sleep home here one more night, and tomorrow morning I decide again.'

"And now every morning Deep Red Roses decides with her head to take the clock. She takes the clock and starts away and then comes back because her heart decides she must have the looking glass.

"If you go to her house this morning you will see her standing in the doorway with blue skylights like the blue sky of early April in her eyes, and lips that remind you of deep red roses in the cool of the evening in summer. You will see her leave the doorway and go out of the gate with the clock in her hands. Then if you wait you will see her come back through the gate, into the door, back to her room where she puts down the clock and takes up the looking glass.

"After that she decides to wait until tomorrow morning to decide again what to decide. Her head tells her one thing, her heart tells her another. Between the two she stays home. Sometimes she looks at her face in the looking glass and says to herself, 'I am young yet and while I am young I am going to do my own deciding.' "

Blixie Bimber fingered the end of her chin with her little finger and said, "It is a strange story. It has a stab in it. It would hurt me if I couldn't look up at the big white clouds shouldering their shoulders, rolling on the rollers of the big blue sky."

"It is a good story to tell when April is here all over again—and I am shining up the brass bickerjiggers on my accordion," said the Potato Face Blind Man.

*How Hot Balloons and His
Pigeon Daughters Crossed
Over into the Rootabaga
Country*

HOT Balloons was a man who
lived all alone among people
who sell slips, flips, flicks, and chicks

by the dozen, by the box, by the box car job lot, back and forth to each other.

Hot Balloons used to open the window in the morning and say to the rag pickers and the rag handlers, "Far, far away the pigeons are calling; far, far away the white wings are dipping in the blue, in the sky blue."

And the rag pickers and the rag handlers looked up from their rag bags and said, "Far, far away the rags are flying; far, far away the rags are whistling in the wind, in the sky wind."

Now two pigeons came walking up to the door, the door knob, and the door bell under the window of Hot Balloons. One of the pigeons rang the bell. The other pigeon, too, stepped up to the bell and gave it a ring.

Then they waited, tying the shoe strings on their shoes and the bonnet

One of the pigeons rang the bell.

strings under their chins, while they waited.

Hot Balloons opened the door. And they flew into his hands, one pigeon apiece in each of his hands, flipping and fluttering their wings, calling, "Ka loo, ka loo, ka lo, ka lo," leaving a letter in his hands and then flying away fast.

Hot Balloons stepped out on the front steps to read the letter where the light was good in the daylight because it was so early in the morning. The letter was on paper scribbled over in pigeon foot blue handwriting with many secrets and syllables.

After Hot Balloons read the letter, he said to himself, "I wonder if those two pigeons are my two runaway daughters, Dippy the Wisp and Slip Me Liz. When they ran away they said they would cross the Shampoo River

and go away into the Rootabaga
Country to live. And I have heard it is
a law of the Rootabaga Country
whenever a girl crosses the Shampoo
River to come back where she used to
be, she changes into a pigeon—and she
stays a pigeon till she crosses back over
the Shampoo River into the Rootabaga Country again."

And he shaded his eyes with his
hands and looked far, far away in the
blue, in the sky blue. And by looking
long and hard he saw far, far away in
the sky blue, the two white pigeons
dipping their wings in the blue, flying
fast, circling and circling higher and
higher, toward the Shampoo River,
toward the Rootabaga Country.

"I wonder, I guess, I think so," he
said to himself, "I wonder, I think so,
it must be those two pigeons are my

two runaway daughters, my two girls, Dippy the Wisp and Slip Me Liz."

He took out the letter and read it again right side up, upside down, back and forth. "It is the first time I ever read pigeon foot blue handwriting," he said to himself. And the way he read the letter, it said to him:

Daddy, daddy, daddy, come home to us in the Rootabaga Country where the pigeons call ka loo, ka loo, ka lo, ka lo, where the squirrels carry ladders and the wildcats ask riddles and the fish jump out of the rivers and speak to the frying pans, where the baboons take care of the babies and the black cats come and go in orange and gold stockings, where the birds wear rose and purple hats on Monday afternoons up in the skylights in the evening.

(SIGNED)   DIPPY THE WISP,
SLIP ME LIZ.

And reading the letter a second time, Hot Balloons said to himself, "No wonder it is scribbled over the paper in pigeon foot blue handwriting. No wonder it is full of secrets and syllables."

So he jumped into a shirt and a necktie, he jumped into a hat and a vest, and he jumped into a steel car, starting with a snizz and a snoof till it began running smooth and even as a catfoot.

"I will ride to the Shampoo River faster than two pigeons fly," he said. "I will be there."

Which he was. He got there before the two pigeons. But it was no use. For the rain and the rainstorm was working—and the rain and the rainstorm tore down and took and washed away the steel bridge over the Shampoo River.

"Now there is only an air bridge to cross on, and a *steel* car drops down, falls off, falls through, if it runs on an *air* bridge," he said.

So he was all alone with the rain and the rainstorm all around him—and far as he could see by shading his eyes and looking, there was only the rain and the rainstorm across the river—and the *air* bridge.

While he waited for the rain and the rainstorm to go down, two pigeons came flying into his hands, one apiece into each hand, flipping and fluttering their wings and calling, "Ka loo, ka loo, ka lo, ka lo." And he could tell by the way they began tying the shoe-strings on their shoes and the bonnet strings under their chins, they were the same two pigeons ringing the door bell that morning.

They wrote on his thumbnails in pigeon foot blue handwriting, and he read their handwriting asking him why he didn't cross over the Shampoo River. And he explained, "There is only an *air* bridge to cross on. A *steel* car drops down, falls off, falls through, if it runs on an *air* bridge. Change my *steel* car to an *air* car. Then I can cross the *air* bridge."

The pigeons flipped and fluttered, dipped their wings and called, "Ka loo, ka loo, ka lo, ka lo." And they scribbled their pigeon feet on his thumbnail—telling him to wait. So the pigeons went flying across the Shampoo River.

They came back with a basket. In the basket was a snoox and a gringo. And the snoox and the gringo took hammers, jacks, flanges, nuts, screws, bearings, ball bearings, axles, axle grease, ax handles, spits, spitters, spit-balls, and spitfires, and worked.

"It's a hot job," said the snoox to the gringo. "I'll say it's a hot job," said the gringo answering the snoox.

"We'll give this one the merry razoo," said the snoox to the gringo, working overtime and double time. "Yes, we'll put her to the cleaners and shoot her into high," said the gringo, answering the snoox, working overtime and double time.

They changed the steel to air, made an *air* car of the *steel* car, put Hot Balloons and the two pigeons into the air car and *drove the air car across the air bridge*.

And nowadays when people talk about it in the Rootabaga Country, they say, "The snoox and the gringo drove the air car across the air bridge clean and cool as a whistle in the wind.

As soon as the car got off the bridge and over into the Rootabaga Country, the two pigeons changed in a flash. And Hot Balloons saw they were his two daughters, his two runaway girls, Dippy the Wisp and Slip Me Liz, standing and smiling at him and looking fresh and free as two fresh fish in a free river, fresh and free as two fresh bimbos in a bamboo tree."

He kissed them both, two long kisses, and while he was kissing them the snoox and the gringo worked double time and overtime and changed the *air* car back into a *steel* car.

And Dippy the Wisp and Slip Me Liz rode in that car—starting with a snizz and a snoof till it began running smooth and even as a catfoot—showing their father, Hot Balloons, where the squirrels carry ladders and the wildcats ask riddles and the fish jump out of the rivers and speak to the frying pans, where the baboons take care of the babies and the black cats come and go in orange and gold stockings, where the birds wear rose and purple hats on Monday afternoons up in the skylights in the evening.

And often on a Saturday night or a New Year's Eve or a Christmas morning, Hot Balloons remembers back how things used to be, and he tells his two girls about the rag pickers and the rag handlers back among the people who sell slips, flips, flicks, and chicks, by the dozen, by the box, by the box car job lot, back and forth to each other.

The Haystack Cricket and How Things Are Different up in the Moon Towns

T HERE is an old man with wrinkles like wrinkled leather on his face living among the cornfields on the rolling prairie near the Shampoo River.

His name is John Jack Johannes Hummadummaduffer. His cronies and the people who know him call him Feed Box.

His daughter is a cornfield girl with hair shining the way cornsilk shines when the corn is ripe in the fall time. The tassels of cornsilk hang down and blow in the wind with a rusty dark gold, and they seem to get mixed with her hair. Her name is Eva Evelyn Evangeline Hummadummaduffer. And her chums and the people who know her call her Sky Blue.

The eleventh month, November, comes every year to the corn belt on that rolling prairie. The wagons bring the corn from the fields in the harvest days and the cracks in the corncribs shine with the yellow and gold of the corn.

The harvest moon comes, too.

They say it stacks sheaves of the November gold moonshine into gold corn shocks on the sky. So they say.

On those mornings in November that time of the year, the old man they call Feed Box sits where the sun shines against the boards of a corncrib.

The girl they call Sky Blue, even though her name is Eva Evelyn Evangeline Hummadummaduffer, she comes along one November morning. Her father is sitting in the sun with his back against a corncrib. And he tells her he always sits there every year listening to the mice in the cornfields getting ready to move into the big farmhouse.

"When the frost comes and the corn is husked and put in the corncribs, the fields are cleaned and the cold nights come. Papa mouse and mama mouse tell the little ones it is time to sneak into the cellar and the garret and the attic of the farmhouse," said Feed Box to Sky Blue.

"I am listening," she said, "and I can hear the papa mouse and the mama mouse telling the little ones how they will find rags and paper and wool and splinters and shavings and hair, and they will make warm nests for the winter in the big farmhouse—if no kits, cats, nor kittycats get them."

The old man, Feed Box, rubbed his back and his shoulders against the boards of the corncrib and washed his hands almost as if he might be washing them in the gold of the autumn sunshine. Then he told this happening:

This time of the year, when the mouse in the fields whispers so I can hear him, I remember one November when I was a boy.

One night in November when the harvest moon was shining and stacking gold cornshocks in the sky, I got lost. Instead of going home I was going away from home. And the next day and the next night instead of going home I was going away from home.

That second night I came to a haystack where a yellow and gold cricket was singing. And he was singing the same songs the crickets sing in the haystacks back home where the Hummadummaduffers raise hay and corn, in the corn belt near the Shampoo River.

And he told me, this cricket did, he told me when he listened soft if everything was still in the grass and the sky, he could hear golden crickets singing in the cornshocks the harvest moon had stacked in the sky.

I went to sleep listening to the singing of the yellow and gold crickets in that haystack. It was early in the morning, long before daylight, I guess, the two of us went on a trip away from the haystack.

We took a trip. The yellow and gold cricket led the way. "It is the call of the harvest moon," he said to me in a singing whisper. "We are going up to the moon towns where the harvest moon stacks the cornshocks on the sky."

We came to a little valley in the sky. And the harvest moon had slipped three little towns into that valley, three little towns named Half Moon, Baby Moon, and Silver Moon.

In the town of Half Moon they *look* out of the doors and *come in* at the windows. So they have taken all the doorbells off the doors and put them on the windows. Whenever we rang a doorbell we went to a window.

In the town of Baby Moon they had windows on the chimneys so the smoke can look out of the window and see the weather before it comes out over the top of the chimney. And whenever the chimneys get tired of being stuck up on the top of the roof, the chimneys climb down and dance in the cellar. We saw five chimneys climb down and join hands and bump heads and dance a laughing chimney dance.

In the town of Silver Moon the cellars are not satisfied. They say to each other, "We are tired of being under, always under." So the cellars slip out from being under, always under. They slip out and climb up on top of the roof.

And that was all we saw up among the moon towns of Half Moon, Baby Moon, and Silver Moon. We had to get back to the haystack so as to get up in the morning after our night sleep.

"This time of the year I always remember that November," said the old man, Feed Box, to his daughter, Sky Blue.

And Sky Blue said, "I am going to sleep in a haystack sometime in November just to see if a yellow and gold cricket will come with a singing whisper and take me on a trip to where the doorbells are on the windows and the chimneys climb down and dance."

The old man murmured, "Don't forget the cellars tired of being under, always under."

Sand Flat Shadows

FIRE the Goat and Flim the Goose slept out. Stub pines stood over them. And away up next over the stub pines were stars.

It was a white sand flat they slept on. The floor of the sand flat ran straight to the Big Lake of the Booming Rollers.

And just over the sand flat and just over the booming rollers was a high room where the mist people were making pictures. Gray pictures, blue and sometimes a little gold, and often silver, were the pictures.

And next just over the high room where the mist people were making pictures, next just over were the stars."

Over everything and always last and highest of all, were the stars.

Fire the Goat took off his horns. Flim the Goose took off his wings. "This is where we sleep," they said to each other, "here in the stub pines on the sand flats next to the booming rollers and high over everything and always last and highest of all, the stars."

Fire the Goat laid his horns under his head. Flim the Goose laid his wings under his head. "This is the best place for what you want to keep," they said to each other. Then they crossed their fingers for luck and lay down and went to sleep and slept. And while they slept the mist people went on making pictures. Gray pictures, blue and sometimes a little gold but more often silver, such were the pictures the mist people went on making while Fire the Goat and Flim the Goose went on sleeping. And over everything and always last and highest of all, were the stars.

They woke up. Fire the Goat took his horns out and put them on. "It's morning now," he said.

Flim the Goose took his wings out and put them on. "It's another day now," he said.

Then they sat looking. Away off where the sun was coming up, inching and pushing up far across the rim curve of the Big Lake of the Booming Rollers, along the whole line of the east sky, there were people and animals, all

Away off where the sun was coming up, there were people and animals.

black or all so gray they were near black.

There was a big horse with his mouth open, ears laid back, front legs thrown in two curves like harvest sickles.

There was a camel with two humps, moving slow and grand like he had all the time of all the years of all the world to go in.

There was an elephant without any head, with six short legs. There were many cows. There was a man with a club over his shoulder and a woman with a bundle on the back of her neck.

And they marched on. They were going nowhere, it seemed. And they were going slow. They had plenty of time. There was nothing else to do. It was fixed for them to do it, long ago it was fixed. And so they were marching.

Sometimes the big horse's head

sagged and dropped off and came back again. Sometimes the humps of the camel sagged and dropped off and came back again. And sometimes the club on the man's shoulder got bigger and heavier and the man staggered under it and then his legs got bigger and stronger and he steadied himself and went on. And again sometimes the bundle on the back of the neck of the woman got bigger and heavier and the bundle sagged and the woman staggered and her legs got bigger and stronger and she steadied herself and went on.

This was the show, the hippodrome, the spectacular circus that passed on the east sky before the eyes of Fire the Goat and Flim the Goose.

"Which is this, who are they and why do they come?" Flim the Goose asked Fire the Goat.

"Do you ask me because you wish me to tell you?" asked Fire the Goat.

"Indeed it is a question to which I want an honest answer."

"Has never the father or mother nor the uncle or aunt nor the kith and kin of Flim the Goose told him the what and the which of this?"

"Never has the such of this which been put here this way to me by anybody."

Flim the Goose held up his fingers and said, "I don't talk to you with my fingers crossed."

And so Fire the Goat began to explain to Flim the Goose all about the show, the hippodrome, the mastodonic cyclopean spectacle which was passing on the east sky in front of the sun coming up.

"People say they are shadows," began Fire the Goat. "That is a name, a word, a little cough, and a couple of syllables.

"For some people shadows are comic and only to laugh at. For some other people shadows are like a mouth and its breath. The breath comes out and it is nothing. It is like air and no-body can make it into a package and carry it away. It will not melt like gold nor can you shovel it like cinders. So to these people it means nothing.

"And then there are other people," Fire the Goat went on. "There are other people who understand shadows. The fire-born understand. The fire-born know where shadows come from and why they are.

"Long ago, when the Makers of the World were done making the round earth, the time came when they were ready to make the animals to put on the earth. They were not sure how to

make the animals. They did not know
what shape animals they wanted.

"And so they practiced. They did
not make real animals at first. They
made only shapes of animals. And
these shapes were shadows, shadows
like these you and I, Fire the Goat and
Flim the Goose, are looking at this
morning across the booming rollers on
the east sky where the sun is coming
up.

"The shadow horse over there on
the east sky with his mouth open, his
ears laid back, and his front legs
thrown in a curve like harvest sickles,
that shadow horse was one they made
long ago when they were practicing to
make a real horse. That shadow horse
was a mistake and they threw him
away. Never will you see two shadow
horses alike. All shadow horses on the
sky are different. Each one is a mistake,

a shadow horse thrown away because he was not good enough to be a real horse.

"That elephant with no head on his neck, stumbling so grand on six legs—and that grand camel with two humps, one bigger than the other—and those cows with horns in front and behind—they are all mistakes, they were all thrown away because they were not made good enough to be real elephants, real cows, real camels. They were made just for practice, away back early in the world before any real animals came on their legs to eat and live and be here like the rest of us.

"That man—see him now staggering along with the club over his shoulder—see how his long arms come to his knees and sometimes his hands drag below his feet. See how heavy the club on his shoulders loads him down and drags him on. He is one of the oldest shadow men. He was a mistake and they threw him away. He was made just for practice.

"And that woman. See her now at the end of that procession across the booming rollers on the east sky. See her the last of all, the end of the procession. On the back of her neck a bundle. Sometimes the bundle gets bigger. The woman staggers. Her legs get bigger and stronger. She picks herself up and goes along shaking her head. She is the same as the others. She is a shadow and she was made as a mistake. Early, early in the beginnings of the world she was made, for practice.

"Listen, Flim the Goose. What I am telling you is a secret of the fire-born. I do not know whether you understand. We have slept together a night on the sand flats next to the booming rollers, under the stub pines with the stars high over— and so I tell what the fathers of the fire-born tell their sons."

And that day Fire the Goat and Flim the Goose moved along the sand flat shore of the Big Lake of the Booming Rollers. It was a blue day, with a fire-blue of the sun mixing itself in the air and the water. Off to the north the booming rollers were blue sea-green. To the east they were sometimes streak purple, sometimes changing bluebell stripes. And to the south they were silver blue, sheet blue.

Where the shadow hippodrome marched on the east sky that morning was a long line of blue-bird spots.

"Only the fire-born understand blue," said Fire the Goat to Flim the Goose. And that night as the night before they slept on a sand flat. And again Fire the Goat took off his horns and laid them under his head while he slept and Flim the Goose took off his wings and laid them under his head while he slept.

And twice in the night, Fire the Goat whispered in his sleep, whispered to the stars, "Only the fire-born understand blue."

LIBRARY OF CONGRESS
CATALOGING-IN-PUBLICATION DATA

Sandburg, Carl, 1878–1967.
Rootabaga stories/Carl Sandburg; illustrated by
Maud Petersham and Miska Petersham;
edited by Jonathan Cott.—1st Barefoot Books ed.
p.   cm.—(Little Barefoot Books)
Summary: A selection of tales from Rootabaga Country
peopled with such characters as the Potato Face Blind
Man, the Blue Wind Boy, and many others.
ISBN 1-56957-925-3 (acid-free paper)
1. Fairy tales—United States.   2. Children's stories,
American.   [1. Fairy tales.   2. Short stories.]
I. Cott, Jonathan.   II. Petersham, Maud Fuller,
1890–1971, ill.
III. Petersham, Miska, 1888–1960, ill.
IV. Title   V. Series.

PZ8.S25ROS   1994   93-41102
[Fic]—dc20   CIP
                         AC

LITTLE BAREFOOT BOOKS

Alice's Adventures in Wonderland
by Lewis Carroll

The Brownies' Merry Adventures
by Palmer Cox

A Child's Garden of Verses
by Robert Louis Stevenson

Fairy Tales of the World
Retold by Edmund Dulac

*How the Leopard Got His Spots
and Other Just So Stories*
by Rudyard Kipling

The Light Princess
by George MacDonald

*A Little Book of Nonsense:
The Best of Edward Lear*